For George J. – M.

First published 2004 by Walker Books Ltd
87 Vauxhall Walk, London SE11 5HJ

2 4 6 8 10 9 7 5 3 1

Text © 2004 Martin Waddell
Illustrations © 2004 John Lawrence

The right of Martin Waddell and John Lawrence to be identified
respectively as the author and illustrator of this work has been asserted by
them in accordance with the Copyright, Designs and Patents Act 1988

This book has been typeset in Lawrence

Printed in China

British Library Cataloguing in Publication Data:
a catalogue record for this book is available from the British Library

ISBN 0-7445-9260-7

www.walkerbooks.co.uk

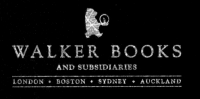

WALKER BOOKS
AND SUBSIDIARIES
LONDON · BOSTON · SYDNEY · AUCKLAND

Tiny's Big Adventure

MARTIN WADDELL

illustrated by

JOHN LAWRENCE

Two little mice jumped out
of their hole in the barn.
"I want to go to the cornfield,"
Tiny said.
"I'll take you," said his sister Katy.
Tiny had never been to the
cornfield before.

The two little mice scampered away through the long grass by the side of the stream. They climbed the knobbly tree.

They danced along the top bar of the gate.
They ran down the post and ...

they were in the cornfield.

They played climb-a-stalk and
you-can't-catch-me-mouse. Then ...

"What's that, Katy Mouse?"
Tiny whispered. "Is it a cat?"

"It isn't a cat," Katy said.

"It could be," said Tiny.

"It's a rabbit," Katy said.

"I know. I've seen rabbits before."

They played climb-the-tractor and sit-on-the-seat. Tiny tried steering, but the wheel was too big for a small mouse to turn. Then ...

"What's that, Katy Mouse?"
Tiny asked. "Is it an owl?"
"It's a pheasant," Katy said.
"Owls only come out at night."

They started playing again. Tiny
wanted to play hide-and-seek-mouse.
He ran into the cornfield and hid.

Tiny waited and waited for Katy to come, but he'd run too far, and she couldn't find him.

I'd better go back, Tiny thought.

He ran back through the corn to find Katy, but ...

"What's that?"
Tiny said,
and he
quivered.

"What's that?"
Tiny said,
and he
shivered.

"What's THAT?"
Tiny said, and
he shook.
"KATY!"
he called.

And Katy came.

"Thank goodness
I've found you!"
said Katy.
"What are those
scary things,
Katy Mouse?"
sobbed Tiny.

"That's a snail," Katy told him. "Look at his shiny bright shell."

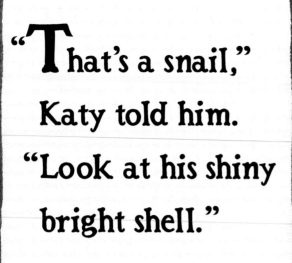

"That's a spider," Katy said. "Look at the sun on his web."

"That's a boot!" Katy told Tiny.
"You were clever to find it!"

They played little-mouse-house in the boot. They played and they played.

Then the two little mice scampered
all the way home.

"That was a big mouse adventure,"
Tiny said. "Let's do it again, Katy Mouse."
And they did.